PEANUTS®
WOODSTOCK'S First Flight!

By Charles M. Schulz

Adapted by Jason Cooper

Illustrated by Scott Jeralds

SIMON SPOTLIGHT
An imprint of Simon & Schuster Children's Publishing Division
1230 Avenue of the Americas, New York, New York 10020
This Simon Spotlight edition May 2020
© 2020 Peanuts Worldwide LLC
All rights reserved, including the right of reproduction in whole or in part in any form.
SIMON SPOTLIGHT and colophon are registered trademarks of Simon & Schuster, Inc.
For information about special discounts for bulk purchases, please contact
Simon & Schuster Special Sales at 1-866-506-1949 or business@simonandschuster.com.
Manufactured in the United States of America 0320 LAK
2 4 6 8 10 9 7 5 3 1
ISBN 978-1-5344-6432-2
ISBN 978-1-5344-6434-6 (eBook)

Woodstock wakes up, feeling a leaf fall gently onto his head and a crisp autumn breeze blow through his feathers. The weather is changing, and it's almost time for him to head south for the winter.

Most birds use their wings to fly south, but not Woodstock. He is going on an airplane! Woodstock is not very good at flying. Plus, he has no idea where "south" really is. Luckily for the little bird, his best friend, Snoopy, is a world-famous flying ace!

Snoopy and Woodstock are both looking forward to the adventure. *You'll love Flying Ace Airlines,* Snoopy assures Woodstock.

But as excited as Woodstock is about the trip, he has a lot of questions. He's never been on a plane before so he's not sure what to expect. Is it safe? How long will it take?

Snoopy agrees to answer all of his questions before they take off.

First, Woodstock asks if Snoopy knows where "south" actually is. Snoopy thinks before saying, *You know, I'm not sure either. I thought "south" was a direction, not an actual place. We'll just have to wing it!*

Woodstock does not chuckle. He is worried that Snoopy won't be able to find their destination.

Don't worry, the plane has a compass, Snoopy says. *Even if I don't know where "south" is, the compass will!* That makes Woodstock feel a *little* bit better.

Snoopy places Woodstock on top of the doghouse. Woodstock looks at Snoopy curiously and asks what type of plane this is. *Use your imagination!* Snoopy says.

Then Snoopy pretends to strap Woodstock into place with a seat belt. *Planes are very safe. You'll have your own seat belt and other safety equipment to ensure an easy and secure flight!*

Plus, you can even wear headphones and listen to music, Snoopy announces. Woodstock grins. He loves listening to music! *But you have to stay in your seat unless the pilot says otherwise,* Snoopy continues.

Then Snoopy explains that airplanes experience some turbulence now and then, but that's to be expected. *You're just passing through little pockets of air. It just feels like small bumps in the road.*

Next, Snoopy shows Woodstock the plane's radio. *If I have any special announcements to make, I'll use this radio so you can hear me,* Snoopy says. Woodstock nods. Now Woodstock is getting more excited about the flight. *Aren't planes so cool?* Snoopy asks.

Just then, Snoopy has an idea. He grabs a blank piece of paper from inside his doghouse and folds it. Woodstock watches closely. Soon it becomes clear that Snoopy is making a paper airplane!

Can't forget the stickers, Snoopy says, placing two glittering stars on the wings.

Now, watch this! Snoopy tosses the plane into the air. The plane flies fast and straight, and then does a graceful circle in the air. Gradually, the plane lands gently in the grass. *Smooth sailing all the way!* Snoopy cheers.

Woodstock asks Snoopy to build another paper airplane. One big enough for him to sit in! Snoopy happily agrees. He carefully places Woodstock in the paper airplane and hands him a small helmet and goggles. *Safety first!* Snoopy says.

The paper plane lands on the grass perfectly. Woodstock cheers.

And flying in a real plane is even better than that, Snoopy tells him. *Nice people bring you snacks and drinks!*

Snacks and drinks?! Woodstock wonders why he's never taken a flight until now!

Suddenly, Woodstock realizes something. Once Snoopy drops him off, he won't see his best friend for a long time. Not until spring.

Don't worry, Snoopy says, giving his pal a big hug. *We'll have the whole flight to spend together. And remember, real friends are never far. And best friends always come back!*

Ready for takeoff? Snoopy asks. Woodstock is ready. He chirps happily to his friend. *Sorry,* Snoopy says. *You've got to wait until we're in the air for snacks to be served.*

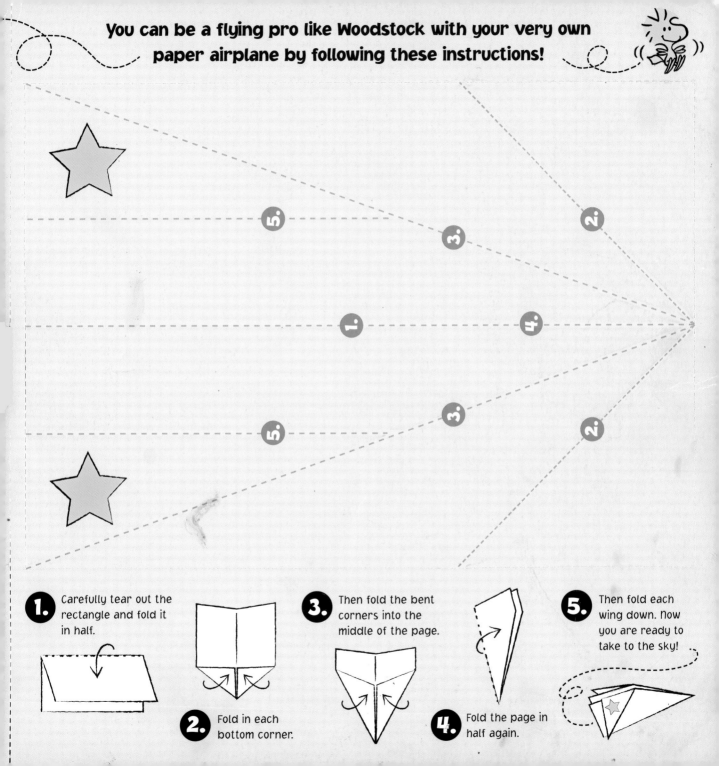

You can be a flying pro like Woodstock with your very own paper airplane by following these instructions!

1. Carefully tear out the rectangle and fold it in half.

2. Fold in each bottom corner.

3. Then fold the bent corners into the middle of the page.

4. Fold the page in half again.

5. Then fold each wing down. Now you are ready to take to the sky!